On Air!

Welcome all you Pokéfans! We've got a fantastic, new adventure in the world of the Pokémon and Johto Champions League in store for you! If you want to be the best, get set to catch them all!

It would be just another day in Goldenrod City if Jessie, James and Meowth hadn't mistaken the Pokétalk Radio for a shopping centre. "Disguised like this, no one will stop us," they say.

Instead, after rummaging through the archive looking for something to eat, a security guard discovers the trio and, mistaking them for ventriloquists, drags them to the studios.

4

What fun going on air pretending that Meowth is a dummy! Mary, the DJ, doesn't suspect a thing. "I've never met such talented ventriloquists before," she praises them while on the air.

5

But Ash and Pikachu, who've just won a battle against another Pokémon trainer, are at the Pokétalk studios too, and are interviewed by Mary shortly afterwards.

The program producer discovers that the tapes of the radio drama, which should have been aired next, have been damaged. There's not enough time to make other tapes!

Mary comes up with a solution: let Ash, Brock and Misty do the show live with Team Rocket's help. "Thank goodness we're disguised, or Ash would recognise us," James murmurs.

And so, since neither Ash nor the others suspected the true identities of the phoney ventriloquists, the radio drama starts. It's an exciting story about some heroes who have to contend with...

...a wicked king and queen who steal a magical stone and cause a lot of trouble. Even though Mary, the program director, is begging them not to, Team Rocket changes the script...

...and make Ash and his friends nervous. However, they manage to turn the story in their favour. But Jessie, James and Meowth won't stand for it and take off their disguise!

Team Rocket kidnaps Pikachu and tries to escape. Ash, Brock and Misty chase after them while Mary continues with the program, pretending that the events are part of the show.

12

On the roof of the building it looks like Jessie, James and Meowth are sure to win. They've already taken off aboard their usual balloon. But Ash throws Chikorita...

13

...and the brave Pokémon shows it fully deserves its trainer's confidence. With incredible skill Chikorita fends off Arbok's attacks and fights back by throwing Razor Leaf!

The first one to get hit is Arbok, who gets knocked out almost right away. Then something makes a hole in the balloon and the ropes get cut. "We're in a lot of trouble, James," Jessie remarks.

When the balloon's basket turns on its side, James drops the cage Pikachu is in. The freed Pokémon attacks and sends Team Rocket flying into orbit.

16

"Glad to hug you again, my friend," Ash exclaims excitedly. But Mary is pleased too: with all these unexpected events, the live radio drama was an incredible success.

The Bug stops here

17

There's a tournament at the National Park and Ash rushes to sign up. The purpose of the competition is to capture the best Pokémon beetle. Ash's good friend Casey is competing in the tournament.

"Looks like Casey's Chikorita is really clever!" Ash thinks. "This time Pikachu will have to do his best if we want to win the Pokémon and the stone prize."

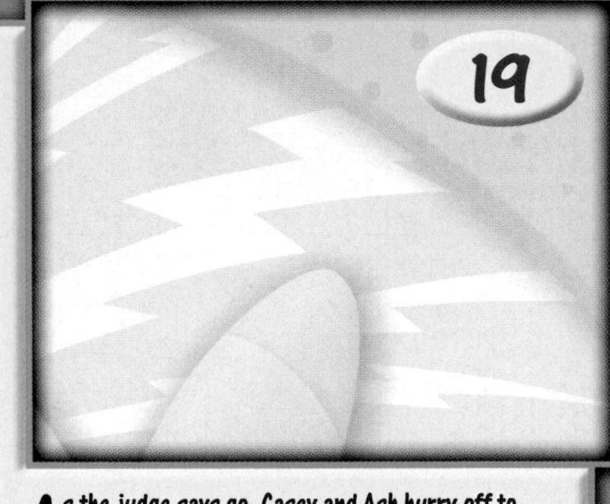

19

As the judge says go, Casey and Ash hurry off to start hunting. Misty, who doesn't like the Pokémon beetle, stays beside Brock holding little Togepi in her arms.

20

Looks like Ash is lucky today, because as soon as the trainer goes into the forest a nice Weedle peeps out of a dense bush.

21

"I can't wait to throw it a Poké Ball," Ash exclaims without taking his eyes off his prey. "Pika!" shouts Pikachu. The Weedle makes sure it doesn't lose sight of its two opponents.

22

But Casey is nearby, and while the Weedle is watching Ash and Pikachu, Casey sneaks up on it from behind and surprises and traps it with a precise throw of one of her Poké Balls.

23

"Gotcha!" the young trainer shouts. Ash insists that he'd seen it first. Then realising that it isn't enough to see a Pokémon, he had to capture it, he drops the matter and starts looking again.

24

In the meantime, not far away Team Rocket has been keeping busy. Hoping to capture a Venomoth, Jessie has followed James' advice and is disguised as a Pokémon.

25

But things don't go the way she hoped: a curious Venomoth approaches the trio, but after a quick glance, realises the trick and dashes off leaving behind a trail of stun spores.

26

After running into a group of Pineco, Casey throws Chikorita again. The rhythm of the battle is picking up and although it's tired and up against several opponents, in the end Chikorita wins again.

27

No break for our heroes! Casey glimpses a Scyther and makes the mistake of throwing Chikorita, who by now is completely exhausted. Luckily Ash jumps in and drives the Scyther away with Pikachu's help.

28

Disappointed with its trainer for risking its life with overwork, Chikorita rushes off into the woods where it is found by Misty's Togepi.

29

While Casey is making up with Chikorita, Ash and Pikachu capture a Beedrill. Right after that, however, they are trapped by Team Rocket. "We're in real trouble!" Ash exclaims as he shakes the bars in vain.

30

Team Rocket's yellow balloon quickly gains altitude. "Who cares about the tournament? At last we've captured Pikachu!" Jessie rejoices, enjoying the sweet taste of victory!

31

Instead, the bitter taste of defeat was awaiting the trio once again. A Pokémon never forgets someone who saves its life, so Chikorita evolves into Bayleef and frees its pals.

32

"Go, Pikachu!" Ash says smiling, pointing at the balloon. "You know what to do!" The Pokémon doesn't need to hear those words again: just one phenomenal electric shock and Team Rocket goes into orbit.

33

Ash wins the contest for capturing the Beedrill but he hasn't forgotten that Casey helped him, so he gives her his prize. This just goes to show that it's not only Pokémon that have a good memory!

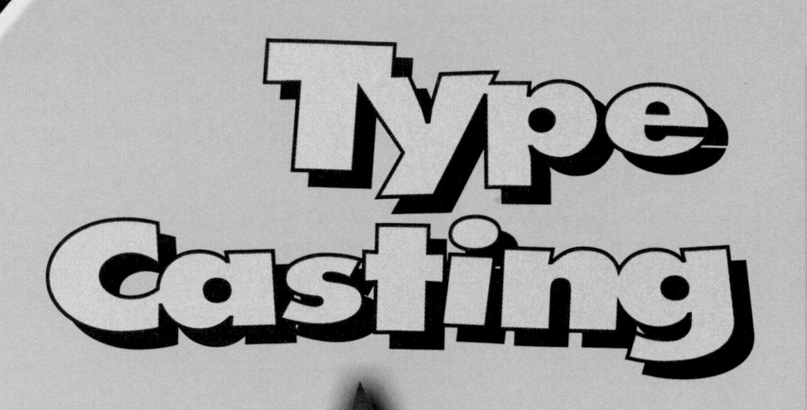

34

"Calm down, it'll be ready in six months at most!" the engineer answers Brock, who is enquiring about the new bridge. The old one was washed away by a storm!

"Six months is too long!" Brock mumbles, looking at the river blocking his way. So Ash asks a fisherman for a ride to the other side and the man agrees, in exchange for a Sudowoodo.

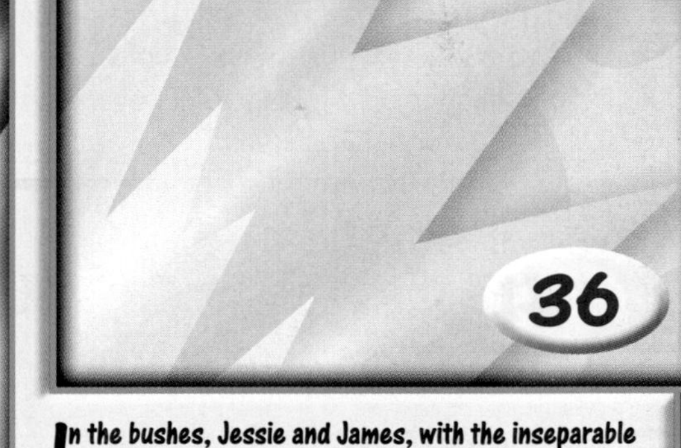

In the bushes, Jessie and James, with the inseparable Meowth, are plotting: "If we find that Sudowoodo first, the fisherman will take us to the other side of the river!"

Soon afterwards, in the forest beside the river, Misty unleashes a Psyduck. But it doesn't take this Pokémon with its psychokinetic powers long to track down a real Sudowoodo. Unfortunately, it manages to escape.

38

The area is inaccessible but strangely though, it seems very crowded today. Our friends run into two biologists, who are also looking for a Sudowoodo.

Although it's a rock-type Pokémon, it looks so much like a tree that it easily manages to hide in the woods. But Noctowl has very good eyesight: here it is!

After calling Noctowl, Ash then throws Chikorita. After trying to escape again, the Sudowoodo accepts the challenge of the battle and manages to fend off its opponent by imitating its rival's powers.

But Ash refuses to give up! A Poké Ball whips through the air and a Totodile appears. Once again the Sudowoodo imitates its opponent and with the same agility fends off every attack.

Team Rocket appears, taking everyone by surprise: who would have imagined that Jessie and James were disguised as trees? After trapping the Pokémon, the Team escapes towards the river.

"So, this is what a Sudowoodo looks like," the old fisherman says amazed, as he stares at the strange Pokémon. "It certainly doesn't look like it's in very good shape."

"A sprinkling of water and it'll be as good as new," the boy explains. But ignorance doesn't pay, because James has no idea that he's dealing with a rock-type Pokémon, a species known to be terrified of water.

The Sudowoodo's escape doesn't last long. Ash throws Cyndaquil, which blocks its route, while wicked Arbok, one of Team Rocket's favourite Pokémon, prevents its retreat.

"That Pokémon is certainly an overmatch!" Ash comments impressed. The fugitive fends off the attacks and first defeats Arbok and then Cyndaquil by imitating the powers of its opponents.

"I've got it!" Ash lights up. A quick Poké Ball and Poliwhirl comes into play. The trainer is not wrong because a rock-type Pokémon would never dare to imitate a water-type opponent.

48

After Poliwhirl manages to tame the Sudowoodo, with just a spray of water it also gets rid of Jessie, James and Meowth and the newcomer, Wobbuffett. "Let's go!" Ash exclaims. "Someone's waiting for us."

49

After satisfying the fisherman's curiosity again, the Sudowoo is freed and Ash and his companions climb into the boat at last. "Goodbye, friends!" our heroes shout, as they take leave of the biologists.

Fossil Fools

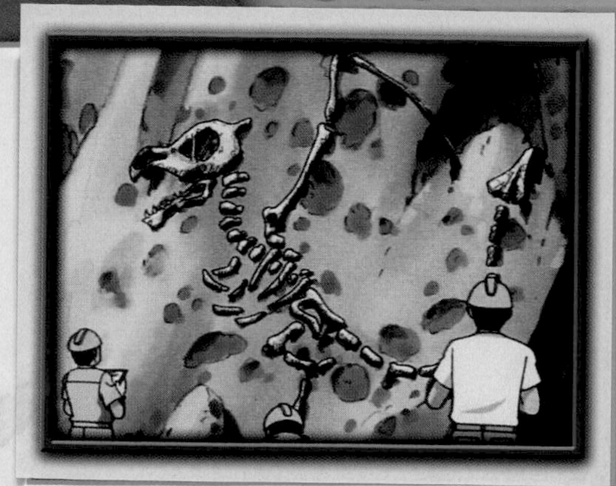

Our heroes arrive at an archaeological site. Curious, they decide to take a tour. "Look!" Brock suddenly exclaims, pointing at an enormous fossil. "Who knows which Pokémon it is?"

"I believe it is an Aerodactyl..." Ash responds, after checking his faithful Pokédex. "Yes, that's right!" replies a surprised Professor Oak, the director of the excavation and a long-time friend of our heroes.

"It was a ferocious prehistoric Pokémon, and like its contemporaries, has been extinct for thousands of years!" Oak concludes. "If it really was so ferocious, I certainly can't say that I'm sorry," Misty chimes in.

53

Meanwhile Team Rocket is up to something on the other side of a nearby pond. "If we sell the lake water we'll make enough to eat until we're full!" Meowth rejoices.

54

Unaware of this, Ash and his friends get acquainted with Foster, a very good pupil of the professor. Foster offers to show them the newly completed reconstruction of a prehistoric garden.

"We recreated a perfect corner of primitive nature on the shore of this lake!" exclaims Foster. "But while the plants are real, the Kabutops is extinct so that's only a statue!"

56

"Which is the oldest Pokémon still living?" asks Ash. "Well …" answers Oak, while some strange creatures start coming out of the lake. "They say some Omanyte still exist, but I don't believe it!"

57

"And what are those, then?" says Misty, turning pale, the first to notice the new arrivals. Oak and Foster can't believe their eyes: two Omanyte and an Omastar in flesh and shell! Incredible!

58

At that very moment, on the far shore of the lake, Jessie and James are having problems of their own. The water suction pump is so powerful that it has sucked up several Omanyte, trapping them!

59

"We'll get rich!" shouts Meowth excitedly, recognising them. "They're so rare, we can sell them for their weight in gold!" James dashes to get the balloon to take them away, but Noctowl is watching.

60

Warned by the faithful Pokémon, Ash, Misty Brock, Foster and Professor Oak rush over to Team Rocket. "Free them!" they order. "We won't let you destroy this miracle of nature!"

61

The only response from Jessie, James and Meowth is to jump into the balloon and take off. In an attempt to protect the loot and help their trainers escape, Arbok and Weesing leap on our heroes.

62

Ash reacts by releasing Pikachu. After some difficulty, the electric Pokémon manages to knock out both the opponents with a single, tremendous 100,000 volt electric shock!

63

In the meantime, the weight of too many Omanyte loaded onto the balloon slows down the ascent. But greedy Jessie refuses to give up any of the captured Pokémon to lighten the craft.

64

Noctowl uses its speed to catch up with Team Rocket and then it thrusts its beak into their balloon, puncturing it and sending the balloon crashing onto the shore of the lake!

65

The three worried villains just have time to murmur "Uh-oh!" as they see the line of Omanyte and Omastar waiting for them. Then a powerful jet of coral water sends Jessie, James and Meowth into orbit.

66

"Go, you're free!" shout Foster and the others, to encourage those creatures that are witnesses to a far off era. And the primitive Pokémon slowly return to the lake.

Hassle in the Castle!

67

When the storm broke, taking Ash, Misty, Brock, Pikachu and Togepi by surprise, it didn't look as though it would last long. And so, seeing a castle in the distance, the five hurried to reach it.

68

"What a strange place!" comments Ash while, in the dry at last, he explores the enormous halls with his friends. "The door was open but judging by the lack of dust, it's my guess someone lives here!"

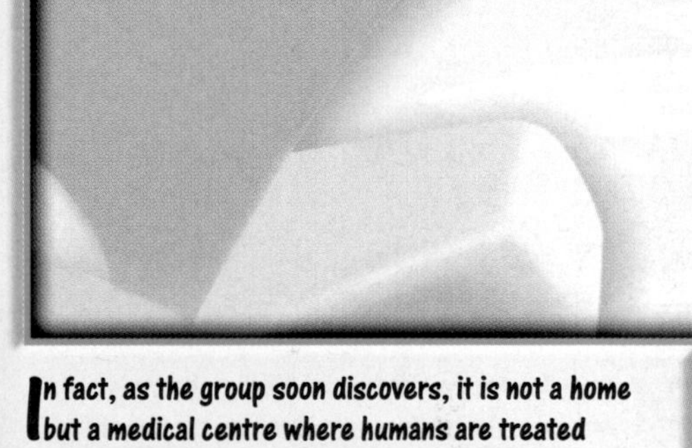

69

In fact, as the group soon discovers, it is not a home but a medical centre where humans are treated with the help of the Pokémon. A strong Machoke does massages…

70

…while a Pokémon Bug, like the usually unreliable Spinarak, was so well trained that it was able to use its web to immobilize any kind of broken bone!

71

And what about the passive gymnastics carried out thanks to the weak electric impulses of a Mareep? "There's no doubt about it!" comments Misty incredulously. "This place is turning out to be really amazing!"

72

"I'm glad you like it!" comments the pleasant doctor Anna, the owner of the clinic and trainer of a marvellous Zubat, specialised in analyses and treatments using ultra-sounds.

73

Brock has a Zubat, too, and a friendship springs up straight away between the two Pokémon. "It looks like those two get on well together!" says Anna. "You're telling me..." sighs Brock, watching them with a dreamy expression in his eyes.

74

Meanwhile, Jessie, James and Meowth have also furtively entered the castle, looking for something to eat. Caught red handed and with their mouths full, they run off as fast as they can.

Together with the faithful Zubat, Brock and Anna rush off on the tracks of the villains. When they get to the uninhabited area of the castle, both Team Rocket and their pursuers fall into a trap.

It is almost totally dark and the underground passages are a real labyrinth. Luckily the Zubat are equipped with ultra-sounds: with endless patience, one metre after another...

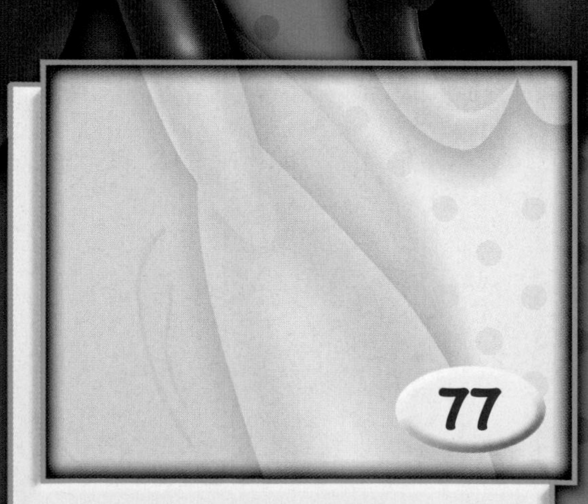

...the two Pokémon coordinate their efforts to transmit the plan of the place to the doctor's Pokédex. "There, now that's much better, isn't it?" Anna sighs with relief.

"This is the proof that two well matched individuals can do anything!" says Brock, winking at the doctor. "Brock is definitely flirting with me!" thinks Anna with a smile.

Meanwhile, upstairs, Ash, Misty and the doctor's nurse are studying a map. "To reach the underground room we have to dig here!" decides Ash, pointing to a spot on the map.

A little while later, also with the help of Pikachu, Togepi, a willing Pineco and a clever Geodude, the last thin layer of rock separating the two groups finally gives way to the pickaxe blows.

"Thanks... for the lift, friends!" say Brock and Anna jokingly, returning to the light with the Zubats. "But... but where are Jessie, James and Meowth hiding?" asks Misty, looking around puzzled.

"Here we are!" James exclaims triumphantly, holding Pikachu tightly. "Now we are on our way, so don't try to stop us!" Brock sends Zubat to attack and Team Rocket bursts out laughing. "That's not powerful enough..."

... Jessie starts to say. But Zubat evolves into Golbat, and Jessie falls silent. Once Team Rocket has been defeated, Ash and his friends leave the castle. "Maybe it just wasn't our destiny!" Brock consoles himself, waving goodbye to Anna.

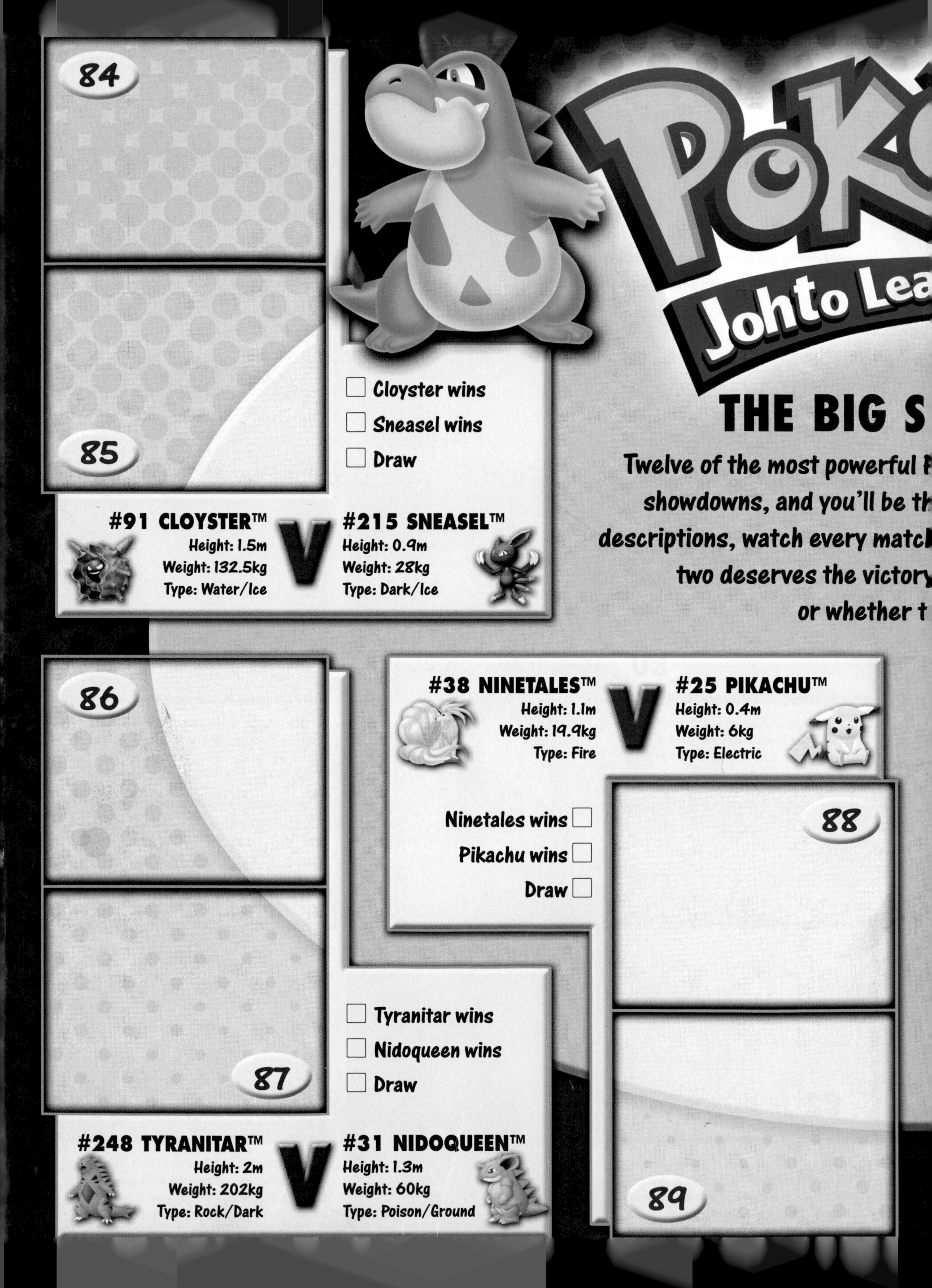
Pokémon
Johto League
THE BIG S
Twelve of the most powerful P
showdowns, and you'll be th
descriptions, watch every match
two deserves the victory
or whether t
84
85
Cloyster wins
Sneasel wins
Draw
#91 CLOYSTER™
Height: 1.5m
Weight: 132.5kg
Type: Water/Ice
V
#215 SNEASEL™
Height: 0.9m
Weight: 28kg
Type: Dark/Ice
#38 NINETALES™
Height: 1.1m
Weight: 19.9kg
Type: Fire
V
#25 PIKACHU™
Height: 0.4m
Weight: 6kg
Type: Electric
Ninetales wins
Pikachu wins
Draw
86
87
88
89
Tyranitar wins
Nidoqueen wins
Draw
#248 TYRANITAR™
Height: 2m
Weight: 202kg
Type: Rock/Dark
V
#31 NIDOQUEEN™
Height: 1.3m
Weight: 60kg
Type: Poison/Ground

OWDOWN

kémon ever known clash in six
judge. Carefully read these
nd decide whether either of the
put an x in the right box)
call it a draw.

90

91

Charizard wins ☐
Feraligatr wins ☐
Draw ☐

#6 CHARIZARD™
Height: 1.7m
Weight: 90.5kg
Type: Fire/Flying

V

#160 FERALIGATR™
Height: 2.3m
Weight: 88.8kg
Type: Water

#196 ESPEON™
Height: 0.9m
Weight: 26.5kg
Type: Psychic

V

#126 MAGMAR™
Height: 1.3m
Weight: 44.5kg
Type: Fire

Espeon wins ☐
Magmar wins ☐
Draw ☐

94

95

92

93

☐ Aerodactyl wins
☐ Lapras wins
☐ Draw

#142 AERODACTYL™
Height: 1.8m
Weight: 59kg
Type: Rock/Flying

V

#131 LAPRAS™
Height: 2.5m
Weight: 220kg
Type: Water/Ice

Two Hits and a Miss

Travelling towards Ecruteak City, Ash, Brock and Misty are taken by surprise when they hear a sudden, deafening roar. They whip round to discover where it's coming from and, especially, what is causing it.

It's Taurus, a powerful Pokémon that is hurtling along in a wild gallop, threatening to crush an old man walking along the path. Ash throws a Poké Ball...

...and Bulbasaur is freed into the air, determined to capture Taurus with its tentacles. It looks like a one-sided battle, given the different size of the two opponents...

...but Ash hasn't thrown just any Poké Ball chosen at random, and is convinced of the ability of his Pokémon. Bulbasaur doesn't let him down: getting hold of the colossus by the horns, it throws Taurus to the ground, knocking it out of action.

"I don't understand what a Taurus is doing in this area!" Ash murmurs pensively. "Thanks, boy!" says the old man, interrupting him. "You're a fine trainer and you've saved my life!"

101

The mystery of why a Tauros is there is soon cleared up: a boy arrives running down the path. "Good job, here it is!" he sighs with relief, holding up a Poké Ball. "It escaped!" he admits.

The old man, whose name is Kenzo, turns out to be a master trainer and leads the group to his Pokémon training gym. Here Ash is challenged by Kenzo's granddaughter, Chigusa...

103

...but they don't have time to even start the fight before young Shiro arrives. The newcomer, a wannabe master trainer, challenges old Kenzo, throwing his strong Hitmonlee into the ring.

104

But Kenzo has backache, and so Chigusa takes up the challenge with her Hitmontop. The struggle is frenetic and, in spite of Chigusa and Hitmontop doing their best, the victory goes to Hitmonlee.

105

Suddenly a net falls from the sky, trapping both opponents' Pokémon and interrupting the fight. "Team Rocket!" yells Ash, raising his eyes to the sky.

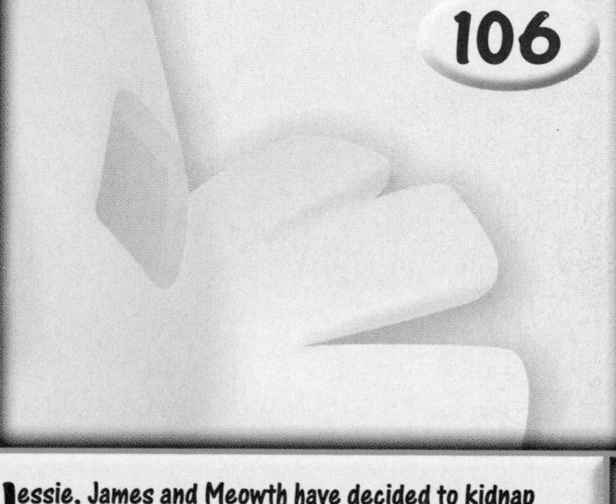

106

Jessie, James and Meowth have decided to kidnap Hitmonlee and Hitmontop. Their balloon begins to rise and they would soon have been out of reach...

107

...if Ash hadn't launched Bulbasaur. Laughing to themselves, the kidnappers are convinced that they have got away with it. However, Bulbasaur quickly frees the kidnapped Pokémon by using its razor leaves.

108

Jessie reacts by using the gigantic Victreebel, but Pikachu quickly overcomes it and then launches Team Rocket into orbit with a powerful electric shock.

109

The fight between Shiro and Chigusa is delayed until the next day, and Ash takes advantage of the spare time by training Hitmontop. Bulbasaur points out all the weak points of Chigusa's Pokémon...

110

...and Hitmontop is soon on the floor. "Thanks for your help, Ash!" exclaims Chigusa, taking care of her slightly stunned Pokémon. "This defeat has finally shown me where I have been going wrong!"

111

In fact, when Shiro turns up again the next day and the battle begins, Chigusa's Hitmontop is so agile and powerful that it quickly forces Hitmonlee to surrender.

112

"Well done, Chigusa! You're very clever!" the defeated trainer offers his congratulations. "Thanks to my grandfather Kenzo and my friend Ash. Without their teaching, I could never have done it!" admits the girl happily.

Ariados Amigos

113

Our friends are camping in a field a little way from the main road and they're just getting ready for dinner when suddenly Misty yells out. "Look! There's an Ariados in that bush!"

114

Misty is right, but the powerful Pokémon seems to have lost all its strength. Before Ash can catch it with a Poké Ball, an athletic girl and her Venonat appear on the scene to claim it.

115

Ash starts to protest his right to the Pokémon, but Brock interrupts him and starts to flirt with the pretty girl. Meanwhile a mysterious invisible character carries off Ariados.

116

The girl hurls herself after it. Then, when Venonat ends up imprisoned in a spider's web, the invisible man reappears: he is a master of the Ninja Academy, where the girl is a student.

117

Ash and his friends accept the master's invitation: how can they refuse the chance to see real Ninjas close up? When they get to Fuschia City, where the school is located, our heroes ask if they can attend a few lessons...

118

...and the master agrees! "Not bad, these Ninja uniforms!" comments Ash admiringly the next day, when they enter the schoolyard, looking forward to the first lesson.

119

In the afternoon, Ash and the girl have to fight each other to try out some new techniques. Bulbasaur fights against Venonat and, in the end, manages to defeat it by overturning it.

120

But Team Rocket is staging an ambush! Having set their eyes on several Poké Balls, the villains decide to steal them during the night, while the master and the students of the Ninja Academy are asleep.

121

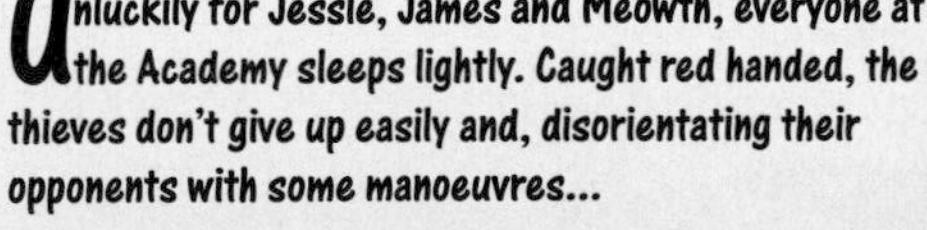

Unluckily for Jessie, James and Meowth, everyone at the Academy sleeps lightly. Caught red handed, the thieves don't give up easily and, disorientating their opponents with some manoeuvres...

122

...manage to take the poor Pikachu by surprise, catching it thanks to some skilful work by Meowth. This time Team Rocket has finally captured Pikachu!

Imprisoned in a special electric shock proof metal cage, Pikachu can only hope for help from its trainer! But before Ash can do anything...

...the master of the Academy leaps into action: tying himself to a special kite pulled by his faithful Ariados, the clever Ninja punctures Team Rocket's balloon and retrieves the stolen Poké Balls.

125

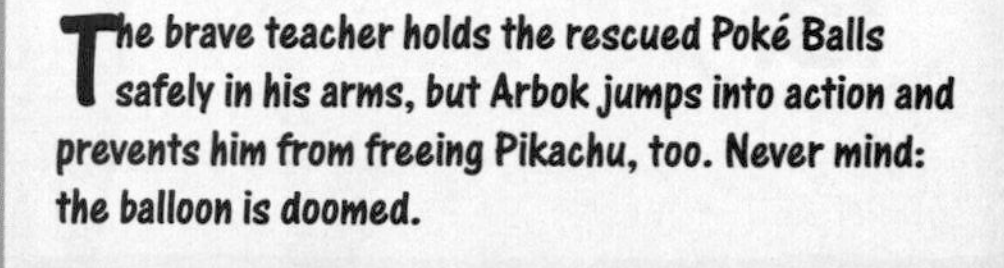

The brave teacher holds the rescued Poké Balls safely in his arms, but Arbok jumps into action and prevents him from freeing Pikachu, too. Never mind: the balloon is doomed.

The balloon crashes to the ground, but Team Rocket hasn't given up hope of gaining victory yet. Meanwhile, Ash retrieves Pikachu's cage, which has ended up on a nearby tree.

Ariados is too tired to face Arbok, and the master rightly decides not to risk it in another battle. So the job of giving a sound lesson to Jessie's Pokémon falls to the girl's Venonat.

128

Arbok makes a hurried attack and Venonat avoids its poisonous spines easily enough. Unfortunately Venonat's counter attack is not very well calculated, either, and the Pokémon ends up in the enemy's coils.

129

But a little squeeze is not enough to defeat a Venonat: with a shower of spores and a masterly blow, it knocks Arbock out, while Pikachu deals with Team Rocket, with pleasure, as always.

A Ghost of a Chance

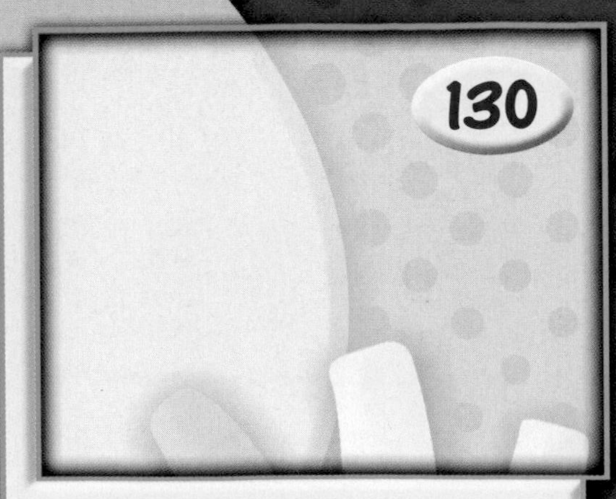

Hungry, as usual, Jessie, James and Meowth are hanging around the city hoping to discover some system to earn a little. At least, just until their next meal.

Meanwhile, in the same city, Ash and his friends discover an old tower. Curious, they enter the tower. "According to me it's been abandoned for centuries!" comments Brock, examining the peeling walls.

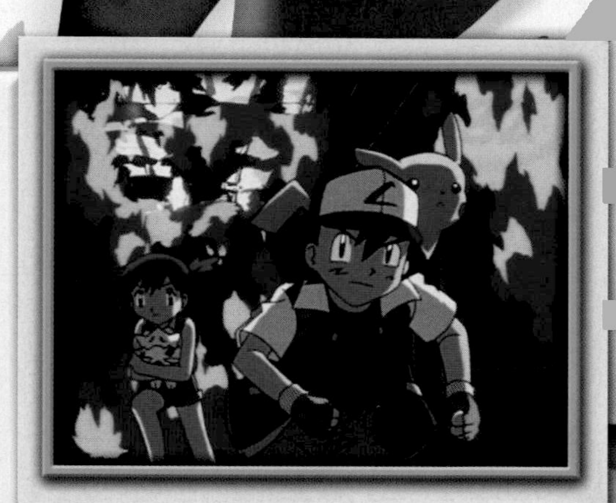

But Brock is wrong: they have just noticed a mysterious presence when suddenly a violent fire breaks out. "Quick!" orders Ash, running through the flames. "Let's get out of this trap!"

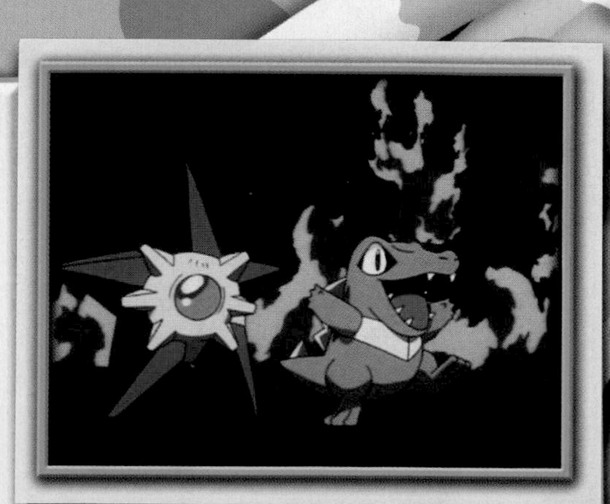

When they can't find the exit, the youngsters launch Totodile and Staryu. "Funny!" says Misty. "Their water jets aren't quenching the fire..." Totodile notices something else, too: those flames don't burn!

Becoming suspicious, Ash launches Noctowl, and with its extraordinary sight, the Pokémon can see the presence of several Gastly in the building. "That fire is just an illusion!" shouts Brock with relief, calming down.

135

"Sure! That Gengar is real, though!" answers Ash, pointing to a Pokémon that Noctowl has discovered. "And it doesn't look very friendly, either!" he adds, getting ready for the inevitable battle.

"Wait, you needn't be afraid!" says Morty, a trainer who lives in the tower and who has a training gym in the city. "The Gengar is mine and it won't attack you unless I order it to!"

Morty shows the friends an ancient work of art representing the legendary Ho-Oh, a Pokémon that no one seems to have ever actually seen. "No one except me!" confesses Ash, remembering the meeting.

138

"Funny!" comments the boy, telling the others that the old tower used to be the refuge of a Ho-Oh long ago. But since the time it was destroyed by a fire, no one in the city has ever seen it again.

139

While Misty listens to the story in fascination, Togepi wanders off and goes through a hole it finds in one of the walls. Pikachu notices this manoeuvre and hurries after the little Pokémon.

140

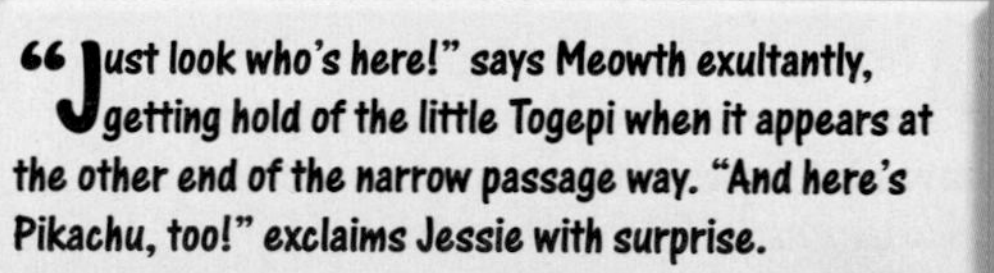

"Just look who's here!" says Meowth exultantly, getting hold of the little Togepi when it appears at the other end of the narrow passage way. "And here's Pikachu, too!" exclaims Jessie with surprise.

141

Pikachu is just going to react by launching an electric shock, but Togepi is already in the hands of Team Rocket, and it would risk getting wounded. So Pikachu gives up and lets itself be captured by Jessie.

142

However, Ash and Misty have noticed the disappearance of their Pokémon and, after a brief search, our heroes bump into Jessie, James and Meowth. "Give us back our Pokémon!" demands Ash.

143

Sneering at him, Team Rocket launch Weezing and Arbok, with the aim of covering their retreat. "Careful! We can't risk wounding Togepi and Pikachu!" warns the worried Misty.

144

"Let my Gengar get to work!" exclaims Morty and, in fact, that Pokémon shows that it is very clever. Gengar defeats Arbok and Weezing with psychic blows, then it cuts off Team Rocket's escape.

145

After saving Pikachu and Togepi with a precisely aimed psychic wave, Gengar finally feels free to have a little amusement: it effortlessly thwarts the counter attack of the stubborn Arbok...

146

...the dark Pokémon brings the battle to a definitive end using an extremely powerful and concentrated psychic wave that hits Jessie, James and Meowth dead on, sending them kilometres into the distance!

From Ghost to Ghost

147

It is only natural that two excellent trainers like Ash and Morty should sooner or later decide to fight each other to find out who is the best. So Ash arrives at Morty's training gym and challenges him to a duel.

148

The problem of fighting against Ghost Pokémon is that they can become invisible. But the Ultra Vision of Ash's Noctowl proves a very effective weapon.

149

Having discovered the Gastly's position, the first of Morty's three Pokémon, Ash recalls Noctowl and launches Pikachu. The Gastly is a master of agility and manages to avoid Pikachu's electric shocks and...

150

...counter attacks hitting Ash's Pokémon directly with a series of precise and very strong psychic waves. The stunned Pikachu can't react with the same precision and ends up on the floor.

151

"Oh dear!" murmurs Ash, taking care of Pikachu. "Those Ghost Pokémon are stronger than I thought!" The judge of the match gives the point to Morty, and Ash decides to launch Cyndaquil.

152

Gastly, skilfully led by Morty, would like to use the same strategy against this second opponent, but Cyndaquil is too fast. So Gastly tries an attack with his long tongue...

153

...and Cyndaquil doesn't miss this lucky chance: quickly climbing up Gastly's tongue, he doesn't use his powers but knocks him out with a simpler, but really strong, head butt.

154

"One all!" announces the referee of the match. Morty calls Gastly back and launches his second Pokémon Ghost. "It will be difficult for Cyndaquil to do that trick with Haunter!" he exclaims.

155

The two Pokémon look one another up and down for a time, both trying to understand the weak points of their opponent. Then, with the tension sky high, they launch their attacks on one another. Cyndaquil starts with fire...

156

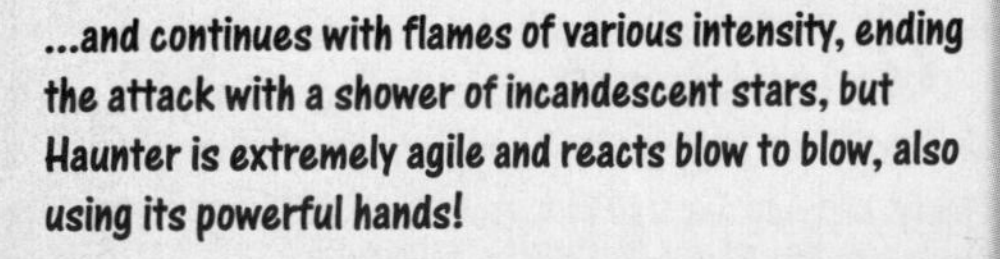

...and continues with flames of various intensity, ending the attack with a shower of incandescent stars, but Haunter is extremely agile and reacts blow to blow, also using its powerful hands!

157

For a moment, when Haunter is hit by a second shower of burning stars, Ash thinks he might win. But pretty soon, it's clear that the Pokémon has taken the strike without being hurt.

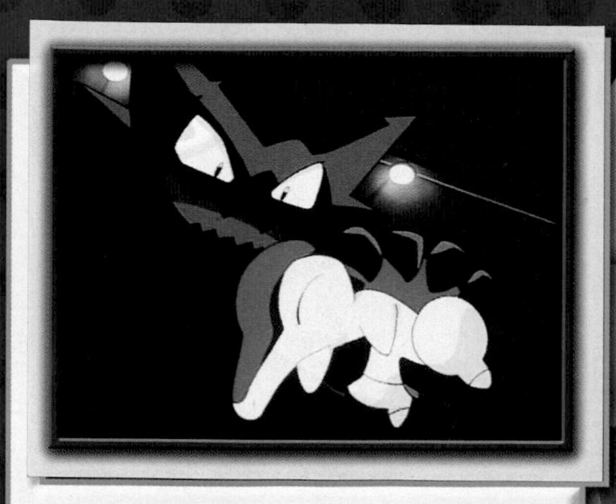

And, in fact, its counterattack is so clear and ruthless that the poor Cyndaquil doesn't stand a chance. Stunned by Haunter's blows, Ash's second champion is defeated! Two to one!

According to the regulations, both Morty and Ash can only use three Pokémon for their duel, and the only thing left for Ash to do is to launch Noctowl again, the only one still able to fight.

160

Haunter attacks, trying to disorientate the opponent with its Confusion Power. But, quite unexpectedly, Noctowl learns this subtle skill and, confusing Haunter instead, knocks it out!

161

Morty launches Gengar, his last usable Pokémon, and Ash starts getting worried. He has seen that Ghost Pokémon in action against Team Rocket and he knows very well how powerful it is.

But Noctowl, on the other hand, is totally calm. Alternately using its Ultra Sight and the Confusion Power, it manages to get beyond the opponent's defences: a single well-aimed blow and Gengar is defeated!

163

Ash is thrilled to bits! But even more than the marvellous medal he has just won, what makes him even happier is that he has discovered how clever and brave his beloved Pokémon are.

Trouble's brewing

It isn't every day that you see an Eevee go past your nose, and when this happens to Misty the girl is dumbfounded. Then she is won over by that Pokémon's tenderness and she hugs it.

"Thanks for finding it!" exclaims young Sakura, coming onto the scene with a sigh of relief. "You don't know how worried I've been!" Then the girl invites the whole group to have a cup of tea.

The group accepts, and they all go together to the training gym where Sakura and her four beautiful sisters go. Of course, Brock falls in love with them all and begins flirting with them one after the other.

But this moment of quiet relaxation doesn't last long: in fact, shortly afterwards the sisters discover Jessie, James and Meowth who have secretly got into the pantry and are tucking into the food.

Sakura is the first to react, and with a lightning fast movement launches her own Poké Ball: Eevee hurls itself bravely against the wicked Arbok, which has been launched into battle by Jessie...

...but courage alone isn't enough to defeat the skill and cunning of Team Rocket's favourite Pokémon. And Arbok captures Eevee in its coils and puts it out of action!

Ash runs to help the sisters, and the combined attack of Totodile and Poliwhirl soon defeats Arbok. The duo's alternating Water and Fire attacks cause Team Rocket to run for cover.

171

"You really are great trainers!" compliments Sakura. "Maybe, if I joined your group, I could become clever, too!" Misty suggests she ask her sisters for permission.

But the four sisters don't agree about Sakura leaving home and they propose a challenge: their little sister can follow them only if Ash's group can demonstrate that it is more skilled in battle than they are.

Ash accepts; you can never really refuse a battle among friends. And so, the first sister takes out a Poké Ball and throws an Eevee into the game, which instantly evolves into a threatening Vaporeon.

174

Ash responds with Poliwhirl, but the battle is destined to stop before it even starts. Suddenly, Team Rocket attacks the group, and Sakura sees her Eevee carried off by a lightning fast Arbok.

175

Misty counterattacks with a Staryu that, throwing itself on Arbok, begins to push it towards the cage in which Team Rocket want to entrap the sisters' Pokémon!

176

While Arbok ends up in the cage and Poliwhirl and Vaporeon hurl themselves against Team Rocket, the other three sisters launch their Pokémon. Jessie and James soon finish up behind bars, too.

177

Seeing how badly things are going, Meowth decides not to fight. "I'll go on my own, I'll go on my own!" it shouts. Then, giving up all its dignity, it goes into the cage on its own, closing the door behind it.

178

Before Pikachu can throw 100,000 volts of energy against the cage, an Umbreon catches Sakura's Eevee in full flight. When Ash gives the all clear, Pikachu jumps into action.

179

"You know, I've thought a lot about it and I've decided to stay with my sisters!" confesses Sakura to Misty, later on, when it's time to say goodbye. "Basically, they're really good trainers, too, aren't they?"

180

Ash, Misty and Brock nod in agreement. "Right! And with time and dedication, maybe you'll become even better than they are!" Then the three friends briskly walk off towards their next adventure.